THE NIGHT SHE CAME BACK

By: Angelique Jordonna

D & T PUBLISHING

Dedicated to Jamie Fast. You know you're getting old when you can say you've known someone for over thirty years. Thanks for the picture that inspired this story and the many years of friendship bestowed upon me.

THE

NIGHT

SHE

CAME

BACK

PROLOGUE

Robb sat on a huge, thick tree root snaking out of the ground. He had his face buried in his hands which were drenched. They were soaked in tears, grime, and blood. He rocked back and forth, sobbing uncontrollably. Robb felt lost. Guilt burned inside of him–he assumed it was guilt. He was trying to process the events of the last several days.

He glanced around. The trees closed in around him, and he fought the urge to take off. To leave everything as it was and just get out of these woods. Get away from everything that he was surrounded by. The overgrowth of plants, the looming trees, the death that lurked below.

"What the hell have I done," he repeated over and over. "What the hell have I done… what the hell have I done..." His voice was a raspy whisper, and his throat was dry. "You stupid fool, she was the one! Now what will you do?" he asked.

He glanced over at the huge hole he had dug in the ground several feet away from him. Of course, this was something he would never be able to forgive himself for, no matter how much he tried. No matter how much *she* deserved it. And he knew there were other options, there are always other options. He had lost it, though, and took things too far.

"I'm so sorry, Donna. I didn't mean to do it," he whimpered. His stomach clenched, and he leaned to the side, throwing up its. It wasn't much, just some beer and chewed up meat particles. He used his forearm to wipe the drops off his mouth. He was like a totally different person when he was around her. It was like something took over, and he couldn't control the urges. Those urges that he thought had gone away several years ago.

Donna could have done anything, and he would have still loved her, but these last few days she hadn't been herself. She became violent, both verbally and physically. She'd been cheating on him; he knew she was seeing someone else. It was that woman she had been with, the one she dumped for him, or she had at least said she left her. It pushed him further than he ever thought he could go.

"Fucking bitch. I trusted you," he muttered to himself as he ran his hands through his thinning hair. "I trusted your crazy ass. Now, look where we are."

His mind was wrecked, and his thoughts continued to jump back and forth between his love for this woman and his hate for how she treated him. He tried his best to give her everything, and it was never enough for her. Just like a woman. You can never give them everything they need.

The night was filled with sounds. Crickets chirped in the distance, and the sound of a creek lingered somewhere in the background. He leaned back against the trunk of the massive old oak, the rough bark scratching at the bare skin of his back. He wiped his cheeks with his hands, trying to remove the tears. Blood smeared across his already damp face.

Robb's eyes were wild with torment. He looked to his right side and stared into the darkness of the massive hole once again. He'd dug it a few hours before and now it was as black as his soul. He let out a huge sigh.

She's in there, he thought to himself. *All alone.* Her blood stained the dirt bed she laid on. It oozed out of her neck, which was now a stump on her body. It wasn't a nice, clean cut either. Robb had used his chainsaw to remove her head from her body while she was alive.

He had hung her from a large branch by her ankles. He watched as her face turned red from the blood rushing to her head. Her screams excited him, and he felt himself grow hard. Then he'd had enough fun with her, and she had to pay for all the ways she tormented him. He pulled out the chainsaw and started it up. She went silent at that point. Didn't even scream as he took that precious equipment to her throat. Small chunks of flesh were still caught in the teeth of the chainsaw's blade. He didn't take his time; he was like some crazed madman.

Her head now rested between her arm and body. Cradled there, peacefully. The lids of her eyes were closed, but her eyes were no longer there. He had removed them when she wouldn't stop staring at him, accusing him of all the horrible things he had done to her, both while alive and dead. Like he was the bad guy, not taking any responsibility for her part in this. Again, just like a woman, always needing to be right.

He plucked her peepers out with a scratch awl that he had in the back of his pickup truck, cutting the optic nerve with his wire cutters. The first eye dropped to the ground, and he stepped on it, grinding it into the dirt road. He heard a popping sound; it echoed in his ears. The other one Robb stuck in his pocket. He would need something to remember her, something to keep so she would be with him forever.

This will be her final resting place, he thought. She always enjoyed the peacefulness of the woods. The shade of the trees. The chirping of birds and other noises from the wild little creatures. She could be one with it all now. She would be at peace.

Robb bit his fingernails, making the skin around them bleed. He glanced at the dirt on his jeans. Blood and dirt mixed, staining the coarse material. His mind roamed, and he couldn't focus on just one thing. Yes, this would be his ruin. How could he have hurt her? This question plagued his broken mind.

Robb jumped when he heard a coyote howl from somewhere close by. His eyes glared out into the dark, searching the wooded area for the culprit.

"Damn woods! You never know what the hell will get you out here," Robb said.

He stood up and walked past the hole without looking into the darkness. He continued to his old red Chevy pickup. Robb grabbed a six-pack of PBR from the cab and made his way back to the tree root he had been using as a makeshift chair, taking a seat again.

Just a beer or two and he'd finish the job, fill the hole in so nobody would ever know what he had done. He'd make it all go away, just like the other times. He tried not to think about those other incidents. Put it all out of his head. This was different; he was really in love this time. Donna was his everything. He could never move on from her.

He popped the can open and took a large gulp; some beer drizzled down his chin and onto his bare chest. He wiped it away and closed his eyes, taking a few deeper breaths. "I can do this," he said out loud. "I've got this." After a few more swigs, he grabbed the shovel and walked to the hole. Robb jumped in.

"Until we meet again, my beautiful angel." Robb spoke to Donna as if she could hear him. He ran his index finger over her lips, and he leaned in and gave her a kiss. His eyes moved down to her breasts, and he placed a kiss on each one. He was going to miss these the most. They were perfect. He straightened her pink panties, making sure she was properly covered, before standing and crawling out of the hole.

Robb looked up at the sky, the moon visible through leaf-covered branches. Strands of light made their way through. He felt a few drops of rain fall from the sky. It was time. He knew he had to let her go and move on. Make his way to a different town. Use another name. Start over again; perhaps this time he wouldn't mess it up.

"I guess we better make this quick, love. I promise to come back and visit you though."

He began moving the dirt with his shovel, covering the cavity in the ground, blanketing her body with the brown earth. He couldn't tell if it was tears wetting his face again, sweat from the hot night, or the rain. It didn't matter though; no one was out there to see what he was doing. By morning, no one would know a thing.

C H A P T E R   1

Robb grabbed his wallet from the dash and opened the heavy door of his pickup truck. He glanced out the windshield at the bright blinking sign attached to the building that read "Just A Nip." He smiled; he loved the names of some of these backwoods strip clubs. The owners always tried to name it something that would catch the attention of the passers-by. It seemed like this time it had worked in their favor because he found them. Or perhaps it was the sign he noticed on the highway while driving that brought him here. It was neon pink with black lettering. Obviously, they spared no expense. The sign read, "No tops and moist bottoms" in large bold lettering and, in smaller print, "Titties, beer, food, titties..."

"I guess they aren't short on titties," Robb muttered as he searched for the exit. Who could resist? He needed a break, anyway. Four hours of driving was enough for him. Some titties, hot food, and an ice-cold beer would be good for him.

A small group of guys came out of the building doors. They were all wearing grins and full of laughter. One playfully pushed another, and he almost ran into Robb's door. His hands land on the surface of the old red pick-up and the guy smiled at Robb.

"Looks like everyone's having a good time inside and outside tonight," Robb said and smiled big. The guy nodded his head.

"There are some wild ones in there. Watch out." One of them replied. Even more laughter erupted from the guys as they continued past Robb.

He slid out of his truck, shut the door behind himself, and headed into the bar. From the outside, it looked like a large, dingy shack. The lights surrounding the building were dim. Half of the shutters that should have been around the windows were missing, and the ones that still hung were a dirty gray color. He was pretty sure that at some point they were white. It definitely needed a new paint job; the whole building could use some color. He's pretty sure it's the original roof as well and probably has leaks all over on the inside.

As soon as he entered, a man on the left behind a thin pedestal, asked for his ID and let him know there was a five-dollar entrance fee, which he paid without a second thought. The man didn't even look up at Robb. He did a quick glance at his license and took the money.

"Enjoy yourself," he said, and he shooed Robb away, still not looking up. His eyes stayed glued to his phone. It appeared he was watching some horror show. Robb shook his head and began to walk away; some folks just aren't people friendly. He always thought that if you work with the public, you should at least be friendly.

Robb followed a dark hallway down to an opening where he was greeted by a larger room full of men and women. Tables and chairs littered the floor area, and there was a huge stage up front. Poles were placed in various areas for the dancers. It looked like the floor hadn't been swept in days.

He took a seat in the back of the room, away from everyone else. Before he could get comfortable, the waitress was in front of him, her perky breasts mere inches from his face as she bent down to hand him a menu.

"What can I get you to drink, hun?" she asked, placing a few napkins on the table in front of him, the menu still in her hand.

"Just give me a can of Pabst," he said. His eyes never moved from her chest.

"A can? We have it on tap, hun. That's cheaper," she said.

"It's not the same out of a tap," he said while shaking his head at her, eyes still glued to her chest. "I'll stick with a can. Thanks though."

Robb finally looked up from those round melons and became speechless. Her brown eyes sparkled in the disco lights, and her smile was that of an angel. Her short blondish-brown hair was kind of out of place and spikey. She was absolutely perfect. Robb had never in his life felt an instant attraction before. That was something he believed always took some time.

"Do you believe in love at first sight?" Robb asked her, unable to control himself.

"I'll be back with that beer." She smiled, ignoring his comment, and placed the menu in front of him. "Try and figure out what you want to eat."

"I can take you back to my truck, and you can be the whole meal, girl," Robb responded, just loud enough to be heard over the music. He giggled to himself, impressed with how quickly he came up with that line.

"Well, aren't you sweet! I don't think my wife would like that though." She gave him a wink and walked away. Robb's eyes followed her to the bar, stalking her every move. He scanned all of her, memorizing every curve, every little mark on her flesh.

"She's absolutely perfect," he said. He licked his lips and began to feel like a kid in a candy store. Except he knew what he wanted. He thought about how this was meant to be, his mind refusing to see it any other way. The wife statement must just have been an excuse. He would continue to work on her. By the end of the night, she would be swooning over him. He was sure of it.

A short blonde walked by Robb, and he touched her arm to get her attention. She stopped and smiled at him.

"My waitress, what's her name?" he asked the woman.

"This is Donna's section," she responded. "Short hair, brownish color? I can get her if you need me to." The waitress looked around trying to find Donna for him.

"That's alright. I just couldn't remember what she said her name was. Thank you." Robb glanced back towards Donna and nodded his head. He knew this would be his new favorite spot. Perhaps he would call this town home for a little while. He would talk to the owners and see if they would like him to fix some of the things around the bar that he noticed on the way in.

After a few moments, Donna came back with his can of beer. "One Pabst, in a can. Are you interested in anything on the menu?" she asked.

"I guess I'll just take a burger with fries. None of the vegetable shit on it. Just a plain burger, cheese, and mayo," he said. "You can toss the lettuce and tomato in the trash, and make sure the burger isn't mooing at me."

"Not a problem, sweetie. I'll get that right out to you." Donna replied, taking the menu, and walked away.

"The name is Robb," he said to her, grabbing her by the arm. She looked surprised by his action, and he loosened his grip. "Sorry, I shouldn't have done that," he quickly blurted out. "Let me make it up to you; let me take you to dinner on your next night off."

She turned and walked away without saying a word to him. He messed up; he would have to make it up to her. He'd invite her out to dinner one night again before he left. That would do it. She would forgive him. He was sure she'd let it go. He could be very persuasive when he needed to be.

Once Robb got his food, he scarfed the burger down, all the while his eyes following Donna around the bar. Watching every interaction, trying to figure out her personality. Plotting out the next move he needed to make to get her. A dark-haired woman approached her, and Donna seemed to gleam, her eyes lit up, and the smile on her face widened. They embraced each other for a moment, and the woman wandered to a corner of the room and sat.

"Can I get you anything else?" Donna asked as she picked up his empty plate and placed his bill on the table.

"Your phone number is all I need." He took the last swig of his beer and handed her the empty can.

"As I said, I'm married. You have a good night though, sir."

"How about going to dinner with me, just as friends? I'm new in town and really could use a new friend. I don't know anyone here."

"I'm sorry. We're not allowed to hang out with customers," Donna said. "I do appreciate the offer though; you seem very nice."

"You'll change your mind." Robb smiled at her and handed her a fifty. "See you around, ma'am."

Robb watched her walk away one last time, admiring the view, and then he stood and stretched. This seemed like a good little town, he would definitely be sticking around for a short time to see if he can make some progress on his new interest. He spotted a small extended stay motel right down the road while driving in; he would go there and check out their weekly and monthly rates. He would only need a short time though. There was no way this girl wouldn't fall for him.

He made his way back to his truck. With several beers and some food in his belly, he was ready for the rest of the night, but his plans had changed. He was going on a new mission. First, he would see where Donna lived, and then he would get himself a room.

Robb sat in his truck, waiting for the bar to close, waiting for Donna to come outside. He switched between radio stations, trying to find something worth listening to. It was getting close to two in the morning, and people were slowly pulling out of the place. Soon, the workers would leave as well. He'd wait as long as it took.

C H A P T E R   2

Donna watched as the odd guy finally left the club. She was thankful that he was gone. He gave her the creeps as soon as he walked in, and unfortunately for her, he chose a seat in her section. It never failed; she always got the weirdos. For just once she'd like to pass one of them off to another girl. They have all passed her a few oddballs since she'd been working there, and she should have the opportunity to return the favor at times.

She walked behind the bar and sat her tray down. She took a seat on a little stool next to the wall. Donna bent down to rub her feet. Normally she does well with all the walking during the night shifts, but the extra three hours added to her workload tonight had done her in.

"I see the creeper has left," she heard a voice behind her say. She turned around and looked up, spotting Amanda. She smiled at the beautiful woman. She was glad that her wife decided to drop her off tonight. She enjoyed having Amanda come in early. Having her wait for her to finish her shift made her feel comfortable. And having a little eye candy for part of her workday was always welcome. She also felt a bit safer with her around. No one wanted to mess with a crazy Puerto Rican, right?

"Which one?" Donna shot back. A little laugh came out. "There's a lot of creepers in this place," she finished.

"The one in the corner over there. He seemed pretty interested in you." Amanda picked up some glasses from the bar and placed them in the sink beside Donna and gave her a sideways glance. "You're not going to leave me for him, are you?" she joked and leaned in and left a soft kiss on her cheek.

"Oh yeah, that one. He had enough nerve to grab my arm earlier. Can you believe that? And he kept asking me out and for my number. He just wouldn't stop. Even when I told him I was married, he didn't care."

"I don't blame him; you're easy on the eyes," Amanda replied. "And I know what you're capable of in the important areas." She had a huge smile on her face. It was just like Amanda, making a sex joke at the worst of times. That was one thing Donna adored about her.

"Girl, we are in a strip club! What do you expect? And you're lucky that's all he grabbed." Another waitress replied, overhearing their conversation. "One of my guys tonight tried to get the real goods. I wanted to break his hands. He went for it and grabbed my pussy. Stupid prick."

"You may have a point," Donna replied, wishing she had some other job where she didn't have to worry about these kinds of things. Four years in college to get an art degree, and what did she have to show for it? She was stuck in a bar, showing her tits for tips. The money was good, but she'd hoped for more when she was going through school. Perhaps a job at an art gallery. A high-class gig somewhere. Working beside some of the greats in her field. Then she met Amanda and moved to a small town. No arts in this area. Farmland and hicks were all you got here. She didn't regret falling for her wife, but she wished for a larger, more exciting town.

Donna looked at the clock. She just wanted to be home, in bed with her wife. Snuggling and watching some little comedy on the TV. Maybe talking or making love. She took a deep breath in and exhaled. "I have the next two days off," Donna whispered to herself. "Just a few hours more, and I can go home."

"What did you say?" Amanda asked.

"Just reminding myself that I have the next few days off and we can spend it in bed." Donna wrapped her arms around Amanda's neck and returned the kiss she received a few moments before.

"Well, I like the sound of that. I'm sorry to rain on your parade, though. I do have to go to work tomorrow, even if just for a few hours. I promised I would help them set it up for an event on Tuesday. I will be completely yours after that, I promise."

"You don't really have to go in. You could say that you're sick. I need a little us time, you know." Donna tried to give the saddest look she could muster up and brought a small tear to her eye. She let the single tear fall from her eye and slide down her cheek.

"Don't do that to me, babe. You know that you make me feel horrible when you do that fake crying shit. And we have bills to pay. Any extra time helps." Amanda gave her a little pat on her ass. "I'm all yours after two. I promise."

Time moved so slowly. Donna found herself checking the clock every five minutes, thinking more time passed than had. After the last customer was out the door, she grabbed some cleaning supplies and rushed to get her area clean. Amanda jumped in, trying to help the others out. She may not be getting paid for her time like Donna, but the quicker it got cleaned the sooner they could leave.

C H A P T E R   3

Robb sat patiently in his truck, flipping through the few radio stations he could pick up. Two of the three were country music, and one played a rock song here and there between all the commercials. It would have been nice to find a good old-fashioned talk program, but his AM stations no longer worked, and the truck was so old there was no way to connect his phone to it.

He started to tap his fingers on the steering wheel, trying to keep the beat of the song. He looked up at the doors of the club every now and then when he heard someone coming out. It was a little after two, and he knew the customers were all gone. Only a few cars littered the parking lot, and they must have belonged to the workers. He played a little game by himself, trying to guess which car belonged to his new girl. Perhaps it was the large black pickup. It would be nice to have the same taste in vehicles.

When Robb finally spotted Donna coming out of the bar, he took note of the car she got into, a black Volkswagen. It must've been a sixties model. There was rust in several spots on the vehicle, and it seemed to stutter a little before starting up. He'd have to make sure she got an upgrade at some point. No woman of his was going to be driving a car that old. He would get her something nice and classy. Maybe a Cadillac or Chrysler unless he can talk her into some kind of truck. But if she was more of a car girl, he would set her up.

The dark-haired girl from earlier was with her. Maybe she was giving a coworker a ride home. Or they could've been roommates. She was certainly not the so-called "wife" that Donna spoke of. He refused to believe that the perfect woman was a lesbian. Not a chance.

His eyes stayed glued to the girls laughing at each other. Amanda reached over and ruffled Donna's hair with her hand. Her head fell back into the caressing hand, and he could hear the girls' laughter. They seemed close and enjoyed their time together. Soon though, Donna would be spending all her time with him. Just a little time, and she would be all his.

Donna leaned over and kissed the other girl, and Robb felt something in his stomach flip. He couldn't tell if he was sickened by it or intrigued. A hint of jealousy zipped through him. He wondered if her lips were as soft as they looked. What kind of lip gloss did she use?

He watched as they put on their seat belts and Donna pulled the car out onto the road. He imagined that she was humming along to the radio and had her hand on Amanda's leg, giving her a wink. Robb knew Donna was glad to finally be going home for the evening.

Robb waited a few moments before starting his truck and hitting the road, in the same direction as the girls. It took him a minute to catch up. He followed them down a long, winding road, its twists and turns taking him further and further into the blackness of night. The trees become thicker and the road narrower. It was so dark that all he could see was the faint red of Donna's taillights in front of him.

He did his best to make sure they didn't notice him, keeping his lights dim as he stayed a good distance behind their car. He tried to keep a good pace, and eventually a blinker came on, and Donna turned onto a different road. When he got close enough, he saw the dirt roadway and a dead-end sign with the words "No Outlet" on it.

Robb drove past and pulled his truck to the side of the road, parking in a little grassy spot. He jumped out of the truck and began to jog. He'd have to follow on foot from here, so they didn't see him. He started running after a moment to keep the light from disappearing, trying to keep up with the taillights of the car. He watched as it turned into a small driveway, and he ducked behind a tree at the end of the drive.

Robb leaned down and put his hands on his knees, trying to catch his breath. There was a rattle in his chest every time he pulled air into his lungs, and it burned as he released it. He should have stopped smoking years ago, but he never was a quitter. He heard the car doors open and looked up.

"You have a lovely home, Donna," Robb said, as if she could hear him. He watched her get out of the car with her friend, and his eyes followed them to the porch of the home. It was a modest, single-story brick house. The outside was well manicured from what he could tell in the darkness.

They stood together on the porch for a few minutes, looking up at the sky. Donna had her arms wrapped around the girl. He knew they were talking, but he couldn't hear what was being said. After a while, the other girl disappeared into the house, leaving Donna alone on the porch.

His girl looked up at the stars once more and pulled a pack of cigarettes out of her pocket. He saw the flick of a lighter. Robb ducked a bit and walked behind some hedges for a closer view of his girl. She would be his, no matter what. After a few puffs, Donna dropped the cigarette in a container and entered the house.

When he was sure it was safe, he began to walk around the home, trying to peek inside the windows. The curtains were drawn on all of them except one at the back of the house.

A light came on in the room, and a bed lay before him. A large room with dressers and a television. Photos hung in various spots on the walls. He did his best to take in every detail in the little time he may have.

Both girls came through a door, topless. Their hands fumbled, trying to get each other's pants off. He stood and watched for a while, imagining himself between the two girls, four hands on him, touching his flesh. He was only interested in one, but he could make it work with this other girl if he had to. At least for a little while. Until he could find a way to get rid of her that was.

Yes, he would find a way to use this woman to his advantage. He continued to watch until they both lay on the bed, breathless. He touched the window, feeling an overwhelming emotion he'd never felt in his life. His hot breath fogged the window, and he wiped away the condensation with his hand.

"It's time for me to leave, my dear. I'll see you soon though." Robb turned from the window and began the walk back to his truck. He didn't realize it was a mile from the house to the end of the road. His running wasn't too bad after all. He would have to work on his cardio though, if he wanted to make this work out. His girl seemed like she could be a runner.

Robb sat still in his vehicle, a smile spreading across his face. He was eager to learn more about Donna. She'd be his in no time. He turned the key in the truck, and it came to life. He would make his way back to the little motel and see if they have any rooms available for a long-term stay. Perhaps get some good sleep; he would see his girl again soon.

On the drive back, Robb's mind raced with all the possibilities of a new life with this girl. He envisioned a little house, a picket fence. Maybe a kid or two. His woman would not work. He would take care of everything. Yes. It would be perfect. He would have something he could be proud of. He was determined to make it happen.

C H A P T E R   4

Robb stood behind a tree staring into the big window at the back of the house. There was a light shining inside, a soft glow that lit up the room just enough for him to see everything. A dresser sat against the far wall with a TV on it, and the door leading to the rest of the house was next to it. Robb's favorite, the bed, was placed on the same wall as the window, which made things easier to see, especially when the girls were in the room.

He'd seen movement here and there today, but no one had made a full appearance yet. He'd been hanging out for the last few hours. Now with it being dark, he knew things would get more interesting as he would be able to move closer for a better view.

The tree he stood next to was at the back of the small yard behind the house. Not too far away was a wooded area that made him blend into the background. It was the best spot he'd found to watch his girl since he scoped out the house a day after he followed Donna home. It gave him a perfect view into the bedroom, especially when the curtains were pulled to the side, which was most of the time.

He'd found himself out here a few times over the last several days, peeking in on his love. He normally waited until the sun went down— in the dark, he could see almost everything going on in the house. To make things better, it was on a dead-end street with nothing else around, so there were no pesky neighbors to distract him. No one saw him checking in on Donna whenever he had some free time.

He watched a figure walk through the bedroom, removing her shirt as she went. She had brownish-red hair and pale flesh. Her breasts were small, too small for Robb's taste. He needed at least two handfuls before he was satisfied. This was the "wife," as Donna had called her. How ridiculous was that? Two women, married?

"Amanda and Donna," he let the words roll out of his mouth. That didn't even sound right to him. He said their names together out loud again and laughed to himself. "Girls these days," he said as he snickered.

He would change that soon enough. Donna hadn't told her wife about him yet. She had no idea about him at all. One day, she'd be open and tell her, though, and they would be able to be together all the time then. Until that time, he'd have to be happy with what he could get.

When he came back from his thoughts, he saw Donna walk into the bedroom with nothing on. She leaned against the door frame and smiled at him. She raised her finger and motioned for him to come to her. Robb looked around for a moment and then back at Donna.

"Me?" he said softly, pointing at himself. She took him by surprise. She must watch him just as much as he watched her. He knew she wanted him; he just didn't expect her to be so forward at her own house. He thought they were keeping the affair a secret until she could tell this woman to leave.

She smiled again and nodded, running her tongue over her lips. He walked closer, still in disbelief. He made his way into the house, and they were face to face. She pressed her lips against his, pulling his body into hers. Her touch was like electricity on his skin.

He'd been waiting for this moment, to become one with his love. He never imagined it would be happening, especially not like this. Her soft lips moved from his mouth to his neck, and he shuddered. She ran her fingers down his back and lifted his shirt over his head.

"Your girl's home. What if she walks in on us?" He whispered. "She'll be pissed."

"She doesn't matter; I'm your girl now. Shut up and kiss me." He drew her in even closer and let her tongue slip past his lips. Before he knew it, he felt her hand rub on the shaft of his cock, and he hardened instantly. It was finally happening, and he could hardly contain the feelings that were welling up inside of himself. This was it. His chance to prove himself. If he could satisfy her, that would be the end of it with this other girl.

A small, low moan escaped his mouth, and Robb felt himself shake as Donna tightened her grip on him. He ran his fingers down from her shoulder to her breasts, taking her nipples between his fingers and slightly squeezing.

"Choke me," she whispered to him. His right hand moved up to her throat, and he squeezed, gently at first. Her hand worked his cock a little faster, and as he neared the edge of ecstasy, he began to squeeze harder. He heard her gasping for air, and he lost it.

Robb grabbed the casing around the outside of the window with his free hand as he stroked himself to completion with his other hand. He glanced inside the bedroom window where Donna and her wife were entangled on the bed, sweat dripping down the other woman's back as she fucked Donna with a strap-on.

He tried to open the window a little so he could hear them, but the window was locked. All they had to do was look up, and they would be able to see his shadow in the window. They wouldn't be able to make out who he was because of the darkness, but someone would be able to see something looking in on them. He wished the wife's eyes would meet his; that way she would know there was someone else, and she was about to lose her girl to him.

He placed his cock back into his pants and zipped them up. He felt a little shaky, his vision blurry, and he had to lean against the side of the house until he regained his balance. He took a few deep breaths to calm himself. When he felt a little steadier, he looked back into the window, his finger tracing Donna's form from the outside. She was now on top of the other girl, grinding against her.

"I love you, sweet angel," he whispered. He took one last look inside, watching this woman and his future wife in complete ecstasy. If things didn't move fast enough for him, she just might have an accident that removed her from their lives for good. He could make that happen. It would be easy to do. A cut of a break line. A stray bullet.

Robb turned to head back towards the woods and made his way down a small trail. When he was sure he was far enough away, he turned on his flashlight to make the trip easier. He finally came to a dirt roadway, relieved. It was about a half a mile hike, but more than worth it. His truck was sitting on the side of the road, waiting for him.

He leaned against his vehicle and lit up a smoke. He needed things to progress with his girl soon. He needed to be with her for good. He closed his eyes and listened to the sounds of the night. Mosquitoes buzzed by his head, and he swatted them away.

He jumped in the cab and started his trek back to his new home, the motel. It'd been housing him for a little over a week now, but he'd placed an offer on a house a road over from Donna's. Hell, it was within walking distance. Just a small river and some woods separated the two properties.

A storage unit now housed all his belongings, until he could get into a new house. If things worked out right, he would have a new home. His girl would move in, and they would have a great future together.

C H A P T E R   5

Robb drove slowly through the parking lot, searching for Donna's old car, but didn't see it anywhere. He eyed every car he passed, making sure he didn't miss it. After a few times through the lot, he pulled into an empty spot and turned his truck off. He sat and watched the door for a few moments, trying to decide what he wanted to do.

"Did that girl bring you to work tonight?" he said. He lit a cigarette and inhaled deeply. "I bet she did. She won't be around much longer. I'll take care of you then. You'll have everything you could ever need; you'll have me. You won't have to work here either. I can tell you hate it here." He tapped his finger nervously on the wheel of the truck and took another deep hit from his cigarette. His eyes didn't leave the door of the building. He knew she had to be inside. There was no way she would miss work.

He took another long drag from his cigarette and stepped out of the truck. He made his way inside the building. The man at the doorway was there to greet him.

"Hey, buddy. Having a good night?" Robb asked. He quickly ran his tongue over his lips as he dug through his wallet, trying to find his license.

"Busier than normal, but that's good for the girls, I guess." He sounded disappointed. He probably enjoyed the slow nights so he can ignore the customers and watch his shows. Robb preferred that as well. He seemed more talkative on the busy nights, and Robb had to do his best to keep his stories right.

Robb handed him some money and his ID as a few guys pushed past him to get outside. *There's no way Donna didn't come in,* he thought to himself again. *There's no way she would call off and miss out on this kind of money.* He was pretty sure the girls were killing it in tips right now. Most of the guys coming in here loved to throw around money, even if they really didn't have that kind of cash to spend. Guys liked to show off, lucky for these workers.

"Hey man, here's your card back. You come in enough now that I don't need to see it," the man behind the pedestal said. His name was Brad, and he was a large guy. His black hair was graying and his beard was growing out of control. It took a few days of showing up before Brad paid any attention to Robb at all. Now they were on a first-name basis with each other and exchanged a few words with one another here and there, when Brad wasn't watching a movie on his phone.

Robb preferred staying under everyone's radar, but he would have to make friends with his future wife's co-workers, so he figured he should start now. Unless he could talk her into being a stay-at-home mom. That was ideal. Have a few kids while he worked, and she could stay home and take care of the house. Just the way it should be.

"Best burgers in town right here, so I won't go anywhere else. Plus, my job relocated me here. Not many other places to go unless I want to drive an hour, guess you're stuck seeing this face for a while."

"Best tits in town too," Brad replied. "I mean, even mine are better than what you find in the other joints."

Both men laughed, though Robb was just playing through. He made small talk to not be rude, but he had other things on his mind then, and he was getting impatient. He excused himself, made his way down the hall, and found his seat in the back of the room. The same seat he always picked.

Robb sat back in his chair and watched the dancers, searching for Donna. His eyes moved about the room, going from one girl to another. He scanned the room again, not finding his woman anywhere. Could she be avoiding him? After the night they had together, there was no way she wouldn't want to see him. The way she grabbed and kissed him, they were meant to be together. She felt it too. There was no denying the connection between them.

It was Friday night, and she was always here. He began to fear that something may be wrong. Perhaps she was at home. Sick and needing him to come and take care of her. Or maybe she was stranded somewhere, waiting for him to come to rescue her. Different scenarios played out in his head. He could be the hero; he could be *her* hero. No one else could protect her the way he could.

He stuck a twenty-dollar bill in the G-string of a girl walking by him and patted her on the ass. That always got their attention. Whether it was because they hated it or were looking for more money, they always responded.

"Hi, can I get you anything, sweetie?" She stopped next to him and gave him her biggest smile. Her Southern accent caught his attention, and of course, just as he thought, money talked in places like this.

"I was wondering if Donna's in; she always waits on me when I'm here," he said, again looking around the room. He rubbed his hands together, trying to get the nerves to leave him. Trying to get the horrible thoughts out of his mind that something really may have happened to her.

"Donna's not in tonight. She took the day off," the waitress replied. "My name's Mary, and I'd be more than happy to help you." She wiggled her shoulders a little, and her breasts moved back and forth, teasing his eyes. Distracting him for just a brief moment.

"She never takes days off. That's not like her. Is she alright?" he asked Mary. He could feel that something was off, and he would get the full story from this woman.

Robb looked at Mary as she struggled with her words. She was a short girl with long blonde hair and beautiful blue eyes. She must've been about ten years younger than Donna. She was a fine catch for any man, but he had already invested his time in someone else. He'd already given his heart to Donna. He wasn't about to start over again. Starting over was always the hardest.

"She just said she needs a day. That's all I know. Sorry." Mary finally responded. "They don't really tell us details when a girl calls off. They say it's none of our business, and I kind of agree with that. What are you drinking tonight?"

"Pabst, can. Burger with only cheese, very well done." Robb became short with the waitress. His eyes still scanned the room. He could feel this girl was lying to him. Donna was not the kind of girl just to call off. He had seen her pile of bills; there's just no way she could afford not to be in.

"Anything else, big boy?" Mary placed her hand on Robb's shoulder and gave him a wink. He shrugged her hand away as quickly as he could, rage beginning to fuel him inside.

"That's alright. I need to get going anyways." Robb tossed another twenty at her and stood up. He gave another glance around the bar, searching the dark corners to make sure he wasn't missing anything and then walked away from the waitress without saying another word.

"What about your order?" Mary called out to him as he made his way out of the room and down the hallway. He waved bye to Brad as he walked out the door, not giving him time to make any conversation.

Robb drove around the parking area a few times, looking for Donna's car again, and when he was sure it wasn't there, he left the parking lot and made his way toward his next destination: Donna's house. He'd need to stop by the motel to grab a few items first though.

C H A P T E R   6

Donna was sitting with a few girls in the back of the club, a small hidden dressing room the strippers used to get ready for their sets. It was just as grimy as the rest of the building. Holes littered the walls from where the owner would occasionally take out his aggression after one too many drinks. A few lockers sat on one side of the room that no one used because the doors were halfway off. Stains dotted the ceiling from leaks in the roof. Why was she even here? She could do so much better, even if she worked at the front desk of a hotel or flipped burgers. It had to be better than this life.

Donna's whole body shivered, and tears streamed down her cheeks. She looked in the mirror in front of her and saw the tiredness on her face. She hadn't slept much in the last week and could barely keep any food down. She was tired and hungry. She was a ball of nerves. She was a lot of things right now, but she knew for sure that she was not alright.

"Hey Donna, you can come out now, he's gone," Mary said as she walked into the back room. Mary sat down next to her, trying to console her. She felt horrible for Donna. As soon as Robb walked into the doors the front guard sent a quick message to let Donna know he was there, she quickly made her way to this spot and had not come out since.

"He really is creepy," Mary said. She took Donna's hand in her own and gave it a quick squeeze. "I don't know where he came from, but this place sure gets all the weird ones. And the way he was looking around the club for you, it made me uneasy for you. "

"I'm so sorry Mary. He just freaks me out. I'm sorry I just stuck you with him." Donna said, her voice a little shaky. She looked at Mary, the fear in her eyes screaming out to the other woman. "Did I tell you I caught him driving down our road this week? I live down a dead-end road. There's no reason he should have been down there. How long has he been following me home? I don't feel safe. Amanda doesn't feel safe. She's been sitting up at night with the shotgun, just waiting for him to come around. This is no way to live."

"Sweetie, I told you to call the cops on him like a week ago." Mary looked Donna in the eyes and put her arm around her shoulder. "He's a weirdo; you said that the first night he was here. You need a restraining order or something. It won't get better if you don't take action."

"You are right. He even approached my wife in the store a few days ago, telling her that we were together, and she needs to back off or else. He's delusional. He told her we've been fucking. If I was going to fuck a guy it definitely wouldn't be him."

"Wait, you didn't tell me about this. Donna, you guys need help. Seriously, want me to call the police right now? I'll help you make the report, sweetie," Mary cut off Donna's rant, but she'd heard the stories before. She knew the guy was a weirdo when he stopped her and asked about Donna. The first time she had seen him, she knew. They all looked the same. The stalker guys tried to be smooth-talking but always ended up just sounding like idiots.

"You know a restraining order does no good, Mary. The cops here won't help until you're dead, especially being a woman. They never listen to us." Donna grabbed a tissue and blew her nose. She tried her best to get herself together, but she couldn't hide how freaked out she was by this guy. She knew he would be in tonight. Like clockwork. He was always there. Every night. He always came in around nine and stayed until they closed.

"We could get Brad to watch you for a few. He's kind of scary. He could crash on your couch and let you guys get a few nights of sleep at least. Give you a little time to figure out what you want to do," Mary said after a little thought. Brad was one of four security guards at the club. He looked at the front door. He stood about six foot five and had to weigh about three hundred pounds, and that was pure muscle. "Brad could turn this guy away at the door. He would do it, he loves us girls. You just need to ask him, Donna."

"He hasn't turned him away yet. He just warns me that he's coming in," Donna replied to Mary. "We will see though. If this guy doesn't stop, I'm going to have to do something. My wife wants us to get cameras for the outside of our house. You know, to make sure he isn't creeping around the house. She thinks he's been sneaking around outside." Donna took a deep breath and released the air slowly from her lungs. She hoped he hadn't been creeping around the house as her wife said. It was bad enough that she saw him down their road.

"That's just scary," Tara chimed in. She was standing in front of the mirror checking her makeup. "I don't know what I'd do if I had some creepy stalker." She put her hands on her breasts and tried to adjust the cups on her studded black bra. She wiggled them and reached her hand inside the cup to pull them up a little. "Do my tits look like they're starting to sag? I mean, they are hanging a little lower than normal, don't you think?"

Donna and Mary looked at each other and burst out laughing at the girl and her questions. "I think I'm losing my mind," Donna whispered to Mary. "This whole thing is going to make me crack. I can just feel it."

"We'll work it out, sweetie. I'm going to tell Brad not to let him in anymore. He can refuse anyone, and this is a time where he needs to step up and do just that. Brad will do anything I ask him to. Leave this to me."

"Yeah, Brad needs to earn his keep, " Tara chimed in again. "He just watches movies all night and takes money. The girls are what keeps this place going. Time for them boys to finally do something. "

Donna stood and headed to the door. "Hopefully he doesn't come back tonight," she said to Mary, and she pushed the door open and started to head out to the floor. She glanced around the club, making sure he was really gone. She'd have to call Amanda, her wife, on her next break and let her know the creeper had stopped by. Until then, the tables weren't going to wait themselves.

"Well, I'm leaving for the night, girl," Mary said as she followed Donna out the back. "I've been here way too long today, and I have a little date. I need to stop by my place for a quick shower to wash the filth of this place off of me before meeting up with Mr. Perfect." Mary wasn't sure how perfect her date was, but she did enjoy their random meetups whenever they could sneak out together.

"Go enjoy yourself," Donna said. "I don't know if there's such a thing as Mr. Perfect, though. Now, Ms. Right, for sure. I just happened to find her."

Mary laughed at her. "Depends, perhaps he has a big... bank book?"

"Eww, " Donna squealed as she gave Mary a little push.

"Looks like he's the right one for me at least. I'm enjoying our time together. No one keeps my attention too long, and he seems to keep me entertained. We'll see." She reached out and rubbed Donna's arm, giving her a wink. "Before I leave, I'll chat with the front-end guys and have them be on high alert for you. And I am serious, starting tomorrow we will have Brad sleep on your couch for a few nights just so you can get some sleep. Heck, we'll turn it into a little slumber party, and I will come over as well."

"Get out of here, before I make you stay and close for me. And don't do anything I wouldn't do." Donna replied and gave Mary a push towards the exit.

Before Mary left the building, she stopped by the entrance and broke things down for Brad. "Please, keep your eyes open. For me. Donna is really worried about this guy and to be honest, so am I. Something is wrong with him. I don't want anything to happen to her."

"I'll do my best, Mary," Brad said through a cloud of smoke from his vape pen. He coughed a little and took another hit. A plume of smoke hit Mary in the face, and she waved her hand in front of her, trying to clear the air. She started coughing and gave Brad the look of death.

"Sorry about that. It won't happen again."

"I'm sure it won't, at least not tonight. I'm leaving... I'll see you later. Eyes on the door. Stop letting weirdos in. They scare us." Mary gave him a seductive wink and turned to walk out of the club before Brad could say anything else to her.

CHAPTER 7

Robb opened the door to his truck and slid in. He'd lost about two hours. He stopped by the hardware store to pick up several items for the night, and then he ended up going to his room to shower so he could be fresh for his girl. Tonight was the night because he was tired of waiting. Everything would play out, good or bad.

He took one more glance through his tote to make sure he hadn't forgotten anything and zipped it up. A rush of excitement raced through his body. He placed the bag on the seat next to him and put his truck in reverse, looking over his shoulder to check his surroundings.

"Well, what do we have here?" Robb watched as the waitress from the bar, Mary, walked from her car to one of the motel room doors. She took out some keys and let herself into a room. He looked at his watch. Did he have time to play?

"I had no idea we were neighbors, Mary," Robb said to himself. He glanced around to see if anyone else was in the parking lot. Robb milled over things for a moment in his head and then turned his truck off. He reached across the truck seat and unzipped his bag again. Reaching in, he felt around for a quick second and then pulled out the hatchet he picked up at the store earlier. He had plans to introduce Donna to his new friend, but plans sometimes change, and tonight was the night for some changes.

He opened the door once again and stepped out of his truck, looking around the parking lot, making sure he was alone. His eyes did their best to scan every dark little corner of the motel parking lot. When he was satisfied there was no one else around, he made his way to the girl's door and knocked. His girl would have to wait because he needed to take care of this first. No one lied to him, and he could feel in his bones that she was a liar. Most women were.

The door slowly opened, and Mary was standing there, a towel wrapped around her small frame. "You're early, Brad. I told you to be here after midni—" Her words trailed off when she saw Robb at the door. "What are you doing here?"

"Hi, Mary. We need to talk," Robb's voice came out raspy, and before Mary could shut the door, Robb swung his hatchet down. Mary reached out and grasped his arm just as he made contact with her other shoulder. She stumbled back into the room, and he followed.

C H A P T E R   8

Mary watched Robb walk into the room. He was whipping his arm back and forth. Her vision was slightly blurry. He continued to shake his arm, like a frenzied dance. His arm was waving back and forth in front of her, and something was connected to it. She realized, after a few moments, that he was trying to shake her arm from himself, her hand clutching his upper arm. She glanced over to her left shoulder and saw blood pouring out of the wound. Her arm was completely severed.

Mary felt panic rising in her, and she wanted to run. She took a step and fell face-first onto the floor. Her body shook a little, then stopped. She was sure Robb could hear her breathing even though it was low and raspy, and she could feel a blackness taking over her, but she did her best to fight it back.

Through squinted eyes she watched as Robb walked back to the door, taking another glance around outside. She assumed he was making sure no one was around to witness his manic outburst. After a few moments, Mary tightly closed her eyes, and she heard the creaking of the door as it shut. In her mind she hoped like hell that someone was around. Someone would come to save her from this lunatic.

"I thought you'd put up more of a fight than that, Mary," Robb said to her. Mary kept her eyes closed, but she could hear every little sound around her. Perhaps if she plays dead, she can get out of this. Or maybe if she tries to scream someone will hear her. She weighs the options even though she feels light-headed. If she screams and no one's around, he will know she isn't dead yet.

A sharp pain took what little breath Mary had away from her as Robb landed a boot in her ribs. She let out a small gasp. "Let's talk about the consequences of lying, Mary. You should never tell a lie; everyone finds out the truth eventually." She heard his voice. It sounded distant, but she knew he was very close by.

"I don't know what you're talking about," Mary stammered, and she rolled over onto her back. Their eyes met. "What do you want to know, I'll tell you the truth, I swear."

The clicking sound of Robb's tongue irritated Mary to no end. He continued to click his tongue at her. "It's too late for that now, Mary. How can I trust you? You've already shown me how much of a liar you can be. No, I must teach you a lesson now."

Mary swallowed hard, her vision getting worse with every passing second. She knew she won't be able to hold on much longer because she had already lost a large amount of blood. Robb knelt beside her, taking her severed arm and slapping her across the face with it.

"Tell me where Donna was tonight, and I'll consider letting you go," Robb said as he smacked her again with her own hand. She watched as he lost his grip on the appendage, and it dropped from his hand.

Mary's breath was coming out of her breath in shallow gasps. Her ears strained, listening for any movement around her. She could hear Robb rustling around in the cabinets. She had no idea what he could be looking for, but she could only imagine it wasn't going to be something good.

A wave of nausea crashed through Mary, and she blacked out. A searing pain that brought her back. Robb was above her, a frying pan stuck to her shoulder. Steam rose and she smelled her own flesh burning.

"Can't let you continue to lose blood, can we?" Robb laughed. "I need you around for a little bit longer. We haven't had nearly enough fun yet."

"I told you the truth. She called into work. She needed the day off." Mary decided to stick with the story; if he was going to kill her, the truth wouldn't help now. Her eyes searched the room for something to aid her in an escape. If she could get a good hit on him, she could at least make it out the door and call for help.

"Oh Mary, you must see me as a fool."

"I swear. I have no reason to lie about it. I can take you to her house. You can see for yourself."

Robb continued to rummage through her items, and Mary became irritated. The little dresser by the bed seemed to momentarily distract him, however. She hated people touching her shit. If she could find the strength inside herself would cut his hands off and shove them up his ass.

She continued to glare at him when she saw him pull out a sewing kit, and he smiled at her. "Oh, I already know what I can use this for." He put his hand back in the drawer, and it looked like he was working his hand to the back. His head turned to one side, and he smiled at Mary once more.

"Oh, you are a dirty girl, aren't you?" He asked her. He chuckled and pulls out a large dildo, running his finger along the length of it. He giggled, seeming to find joy in the item. "You know, I never understood why women liked these things. Wouldn't the real thing be better?" He asked Mary. He didn't look at her though; his eyes were glued to his new prize.

Mary watched for a moment, realizing Robb was no longer thinking about her. She pushed herself up into a sitting position and then attempted to stand as quietly as she could. Her legs were wobbly underneath her, but with a little focus, she knew she could make it to the door. *Just one foot in front of the other*, she thought.

I've got this. I can get away. She repeated to herself.

She was halfway across the room when a hand grabbed the back of her head, ripping at the hair. She was yanked backward and landed on the floor. Robb was on top of her, and had her hand pinned underneath his knee.

"My mom used to tell me that they would cut out a person's tongue for lying way back when. I don't know how true that is, but I know she didn't like it when I used those words against her and cut out her tongue when she told me no one could ever love me." Robb spoke softly.

Mary fought as much as she could beneath his weight but was unable to budge him. When her struggle halted, he picked up the small sewing needle and quickly threaded a piece of red string through the needle's eye. "I see you like to sew. My mom taught me to sew at a young age. She didn't like me going outside, she said it was too dangerous."

"Please don't do this," Mary begged. She saw the needle glimmer in the light as he brought it towards her face.

C H A P T E R   9

Robb took the tip of the needle and started working it into the fleshy part of her mouth. Mary let out a scream, and Robb slammed his fist into her face, knocking her unconscious.

Without a second thought, Robb continued his mission, stitching her two lips together. Small little white x's across the lower part of her face made a horrific design. Little blood droplets formed with every stick of the needle, and Robb found himself fascinated by how the red beaded up and very slowly began to drip onto her chin. He touched the red droplets and smeared them across the rest of her face.

"I guess you're not going to be much use to me now," Robb said to her as he finished up the last stitch. He scooped Mary up, tossing her body over his shoulder, and carried her out of the hotel room and to his vehicle.

"You're more of a waste than I thought," Robb said to her as he tossed her limp body in the back of his truck. He wasn't sure what he was doing with her yet, but he knew he'd figure something out.

Robb slowly pulled out of the motel parking lot and began to drive off.

CHAPTER 10

"Looks like a good night to go fishing. Have you ever done any fishing?" Robb asked Mary as he dragged her body out of the truck bed and dropped her on the ground. The thud echoed in the night, and a small grunt got caught in Mary's throat. "I figure we can do some fishing and chat. How's that sound to you, dear Mary?" His voice had a condescending tone.

It was silent until Robb heard a grunt as Mary tried to speak, but she quickly stopped. Robb imagined a burning pain in her lips as they pulled apart for her to form words. He'd never experienced that feeling before, but he just knew that it must be painful. By now, her strength must be depleted from the fight and blood loss.

When would her will break? When would she cry out and wish for the death that was coming for her? He patiently waited for her to break down completely. Waited for her to realize she'd lost half of her blood already, and there would be no making it out alive.

Robb grabbed her by the hair and dragged her across the ground to the riverbank. Her head hit the ground hard when he released her hair, the thud of ground and skull connecting making him smile. He walked back to his truck and grabbed his fishing pole.

"I'm always prepared for a good fishing night. You know, fish can be picky when it comes to bait. You can never go wrong with good ole worms though," he said as he made his way back to her.

"Unfortunately, I didn't have time to stop by the bait shop before we ran into each other."

Robb waited for a response but got none. The stupid bitch couldn't even keep her eyes open. Just like a woman, wanting to sleep through all the good parts. Robb set his pole on the ground, and he straddled Mary's body.

"I really hate one-sided conversations, you know. It's pretty rude when someone doesn't respond to you." He reached his hand into his jeans pocket and pulled out a knife, flipping the blade out. He was thrown off balance as Mary tried to squirm beneath him, but she was weak and unable to make any major kind of impact.

Robb took the blade of his knife and ran it around the outer part of Mary's nipple, cutting through the flesh and removing the little nub. He repeated the process on the other side. He took his time, enjoying the feel of the blade cutting through her tender flesh. It felt like cutting through butter, and just as messy.

When he was done, he stuffed one nipple in his pants pocket and began to work the fishing hook through the other one. "I hope you know this is a first for me, Mary. I've never used human flesh before while fishing. Hopefully, we can catch a big one." There was excitement in his voice, and Mary retched. Robb watched as she rolled to her stomach and began to gag.

Robb stood up and inched closer to the water's edge. "Beautiful night, isn't it?" Robb asked Mary as he cast his line out. He looked up and tried to capture the moment in his mind. The moon high in the sky, a few clouds floating through the night.

A breeze blew through, and Rob watched Mary shiver. He looked back out at the water, and out of the side of his eye he observed her crawling toward it. She moved slowly, enough that he lost interest, but then a splashing sound made Robb look back in her direction. He just smiled and continued chatting to himself as he watched Mary's body slip under the dark water and disappear.

"I suppose I will have to clean up your room, Mary. You left it a mess."

He cast his line out once more and waited to feel a tug. Just one fish, and he would call it a night, go back to the motel, and give Mary's room a good clean. He had everything he would need in his room. It would be spotless when he's done. Just like any room should be.

CHAPTER 1 1

"Where is she?" Donna asked. "Mary never misses a shift." She took a seat in the changing room and then stood back up. Her nerves were out of control. She clenched her hands together and took a few deep breaths.

"I stopped by her place last night," Brad responded, "we were supposed to go out, but her lights were off, and she didn't answer the door. I just assumed she ditched me."

"That's not Mary. When she makes plans, she sticks with them. I've known this girl half my life, something is wrong." Donna was in a panic now. Mary had been a good friend for many years, and she could feel it in her gut that things were not right. Something was just not sitting right with her.

"Not much we can do right now," Brad shook his head. "We have to work. Maybe at closing, we can stop back by her place and see if we can find anything out. It's on the way to your place anyways."

Donna nodded her head in agreement but knew the wait was going to kill her. Two more hours until closing time and an hour to clean up. Maybe she could talk one of the girls into cleaning for her; that way they could get out sooner.

"Donna, the creeper is in your section again, and I'm not dealing with him tonight. He looks rough," Tara blurted out as she walked past the panicked woman.

Donna rolled her eyes. Just what she needed: dealing with this crazy man while being worried about her missing friend. She walked to the door and looked back at Brad. "Your break's over, hun. Come out and keep an eye on this guy for me. If he does anything off tonight, anything at all, just kick him out. I can't deal with him anymore."

"You got it, babe." Brad followed Donna through the door and watched as she made her way to Robb's table.

She knew that Brad felt bad for her, and she'd seen him talk to Robb several times since he started coming him. He had Brad fooled though; she could tell Brad didn't think Robb was a horrible guy at all. Even with his apparent odd fascination with Donna. They had all seen a guy or two that caught some kind of feeling. It wasn't that strange. It seemed to happen a lot in places like these.

"Hi there Robb. Same thing as usual?" Donna tried to be as polite as possible even though all she wanted to do was to call this freak-out and let everyone know that he'd been stalking her. Perhaps they would finally stop seeing him as a nice guy.

"Yes, beautiful." Robb reached out his hand and placed it on her hip. "This little skirt works for you. I'm going to assume you wore it just for me tonight."

"You'd be assuming wrong, sir. The rest of my clothes are dirty, and I didn't feel like doing laundry last night. So, here I am, in the only clean clothes I had."

"How about you ditch the rest of your shift and I'll take you on a shopping spree, we can get you all kinds of new clothes." Robb ran his hand down and tried to slip it under her skirt.

"What are you doing creep?" Donna shouted while slapping Robb's hand away.

"What did you call me, bitch?" Robb stood up and landed a hard slap across her face.

"That's it, asshole. No one lays their hands on the girls in here." Brad jumped between the two and grabbed Robb by the arm, twisting it behind his back. He started pushing Robb towards the hall, escorting him out of the building. "You can't come back in here, bud. You make the girls uncomfortable, and I've been nice. But touching them is a big N-O," Brad said as he pushed Robb out of the door.

"I'm really sorry; it won't happen again," Robb replied. "Just had a few too many drinks before coming in. Give me another chance."

"No can do. If I see you around here again, I'll call the cops on you. Feel lucky, if someone touches the girls like that, I usually knock them the fuck out. You're getting off easy."

"You'll regret this."

"Is that a threat?" Brad asked, raising his fist. Before he could swing, Robb backed away.

"I got you, bud. I'm leaving." Robb continued to back away slowly, his eyes never leaving Brad's.

"And leave Donna alone. She's not interested. If she tells me you're going around her place again I'll hunt you down." Brad called out to him as he finally turned around to walk away.

CHAPTER 12

Brad and Donna pulled up outside of Mary's room at the old hotel. There had always been crazy rumors about the place, but Mary insisted it was cheaper to live there than rent a house.

"It's all bills paid and no bullshit," she would always say. "On most nights it's quiet, and there's no dirty business going on. And since it's just me, it works out fine."

The room appeared dark. Donna shuffled through her purse, looking for the spare key Mary gave her when she first moved in. It was just in case she ever lost her copy. Her hands trembled as she continued to look. Her fingers finally find the little metal object she was looking for.

"Found it," Donna said as she pulled the key out. "Let's go see what we can find out."

"It's going to be alright, Donna," Brad said.

Donna wondered if he was beginning to feel the dread as well. Did the pit of his stomach churn like hers? She knew deep down inside that something happened to Mary, and he seemed like he just didn't want to admit it to himself right now.

This wasn't like Mary. She'd never missed a shift at work, at least not without a phone call. She'd never blown off a date, either. Donna had known that Brad and Mary had been sneaking around for the last few months, seeing each other when they had a free moment.

Brad grabbed the key from Donna's hand and rushed to Mary's door. He had it open and was inside before Donna could even get out of the car.

"Well, she's not here, and nothing seems out of place." Brad was talking to himself as Donna approached. She glanced around, trying to spot some kind of clue as to where Mary could be.

"Her bedding is out of place," Donna said as she stole a quick glance at Brad. "She never makes her bed. She said it was a waste of time because she was just going to mess it up again. This looks like someone took their time to get it perfect, however, Mary didn't like order."

"The stove's on as well. She never used the stove. I guess it's time to call the police and have them start looking for her." Brad replied.

"Someone really cleaned this room. Look, there's not even dust on the ceiling fan." Donna ran a finger over the top of the blade. "It's pristine here. Why would someone leave the stove on if they cleaned this well?"

"Guess they started feeling rushed at some point," Brad replied.

Brad grabbed the phone and started to dial the local police station. "I wonder if that douchebag Robb had something to do with this," Brad said. "Do you think he's capable of something worse than stalking?"

Before Donna could respond, Brad was talking to the police, telling them everything they knew, which wasn't much.

C H A P T E R   1 3

Robb slowed his truck and pulled off the gravel into the grass, bringing it to a stop. He let out a short sigh and prepared himself for the half-mile walk up the trail. It always seemed to take forever. Tonight though, he would enjoy the walk. Tonight was his night.

His fingers trembled with excitement as he reached into the glove box and pulled out his hunting knife. "Better safe than sorry," he said to himself. "Never know what I'll find down that trail." Grabbing the little mag light from the center console of the truck and his backpack from the seat, he stepped out into the night. He hadn't intended to pay a visit to his girl's house tonight because she was working, but it could be a magical evening if he played his cards right.

He took his time maneuvering through the trees, giving her time to get home and get ready for him. He stuck to the little dirt track, if you could even call it that. It was just a tiny little pathway that was worn down by people walking through there, mainly him. The night was alive with sound. Crickets and bullfrogs played a melody together.

Robb came to the edge of the tree line and glanced across the yard into the bedroom window. All the lights appeared to be off. He quickly walked to the back door and touched the handle, hoping that when he turned it the thing would be unlocked. He never had such luck though.

He'd been inside a few times because there was always a window unlocked somewhere. On most visits, he was able to make his way inside undetected by the people of the house. Hiding away in dark corners, his eyes memorizing every detail that surrounded him. Tonight, though, it appeared he would have the house completely to himself for a few. Worked out for him in the end.

Robb stepped around the side of the house and pushed up on a window, and it easily slid open for him. He grinned. The bathroom window was always unlocked.

"Good girl, Donna. I see you were expecting me, once again." Robb pulled himself up and slid easily through the window. Once inside, he turned and closed it, locking it behind himself. "Gotta look out for my girl; can't let any creeps in."

He slowly made his way out of the bathroom and into the attached bedroom. There was a sliver of light coming into the room from the nightlight in the hallway. He made out a figure in the bed, asleep. It must've been his love. She was waiting for him. He felt passion run through his body.

He found himself crawling into bed, curling up next to Donna. He placed his arm around her waist and pulled her closer to him. She woke slightly, putting her hand on his arm, and her fingers ran slowly up his wrist to his forearm. The movement stopped, and he felt his partner's body stiffen.

The woman in bed jumped up, and Robb realized it wasn't Donna at all; it was that wife of hers. Without a moment's hesitation, he was up, hands wrapped around the girl's throat. Her gasps for air were exhilarating, and he squeezed tighter. He looked into her dark brown eyes, seeing panic and fear screaming at him.

No, he couldn't end her just yet. He would give her some time to think about what she'd done. Trying to steal his woman. His hands loosened, and Amanda punched him in the stomach. He raised his fist and landed a blow to her face; he felt the crunch of her teeth cracking, and she fell to the floor.

"Lights out, bitch." Robb bounced back and forth, imitating a boxer who's proudly won his match against an unruly opponent. He raised his arms above his head and cheered.

After a few moments in the victory lane, Robb looked around the room. Finding a lamp, he took out his knife and cut the cord. "Let's get you set up. Don't need you getting away from us." He dragged her into the kitchen by her hair, pulling her up and getting her set in a chair. "I think this chord will hold you." He said to her as he began tying her to the chair.

"Do you mind if I have a look around?" Robb asked Amanda. He lifted her head, and blood dribbled from her swollen lips. Her eyes were closed. "Don't worry, you can sleep all you want. I'm going to get a beer."

Robb opened the fridge door. He was greeted with fresh green veggies and fancy cheeses from around the world. A six-pack of Corona sat on the middle shelf. "You snooty bitch. Do you think you're too good for a can of Pabst or something?" He pulled two bottles out of the fridge and opened one up. "Guess I'll have to suffer." Robb took a huge swig from the bottle and placed it on the counter behind him.

He looked at Amanda, her head drooped to her chest. She was completely out. He flipped the light on and started shuffling through the drawers, finding tape and some rope. He pulled out a few items to use. *First things first,* he thought to himself as he ripped off some tape and placed it over her mouth.

A metal bat sitting by the kitchen door caught his attention. "Well, look at this. We have ourselves some girls who like to play ball. He picked up the bat and took a swing with it, busting some mushroom canisters on the counter. The crashing sound woke his victim, and she tried to let out a scream.

Robb walked over to her, landing another punch in her face. "Shut the fuck up. I don't like all that noise," he yelled at her. She pulled back as far as she could, and spit hit her face.

Robb walked out of the room and started rummaging through the different rooms of the house when he saw car lights bouncing off the walls.

CHAPTER 14

"Hun, I'm home," Donna made sure her voice was loud enough to be heard, "Sorry I'm late. We stopped by the motel to check on Mary. She never showed up to work. I'm worried about her."

She flipped on the light in the living room and placed her keys on the little table by the door. She waited for a moment to listen for Amanda's reply, but there was nothing.

"We had to call the police and make a report because we don't know what happened to her. She just disappeared. It's really not like her. I hope that creep didn't do something to her." Donna felt like she was talking to herself and decided her girl must be asleep. She made her way to the kitchen; she hadn't eaten since lunch and felt starved. Her stomach made a gurgling sound at the thought of food. Hopefully Amanda left something out for her.

The kitchen was dark, but she saw a shadow. "Amanda, is that you? What are you doing in the dark?" she asked as she turned on the light. As soon as light flooded the room, Donna was horrified by the sight. Amanda was tied to a chair, duct tape across her mouth. She squirmed in the chair, and Robb was standing right behind her.

"Welcome home, beautiful lady," Robb said, and he lifted his hand to show a glistening blade. He slid the shiny blade of the knife across Amanda's throat, and a scream erupted from Donna. She stumbled backward and hit the small of her back on the counter, grabbing the spot as she winced in pain.

"Look there, she's a squirter!" Robb yelled out as blood sprayed from the fresh cut across Amanda's neck. Amanda's eyes went wide as they looked at Donna, and a moment later her head dropped. Donna could hear gurgling noises coming from her. Her mind finally snapped to what was happening, and she turned to run, trying to find her escape.

"Don't leave because of me!" Robb said as he grabbed hold of Donna and slammed her to the ground. Her head hit the corner of a counter, and she saw stars. He forced his knee into her back and grabbed her arms, making a quick job out of tying her hands together. He dragged her up and placed her on a chair in front of Amanda.

"Now that we're all together, I think it's time you tell this girl about your real feelings for me."

"You're a freak," Donna responded. Her eyelids fluttered slightly as she worked on regaining her vision. She felt wetness running down her face, and she could taste blood in her mouth.

"What do you see in her? Why couldn't you just let us happen? I mean… this... we were meant to be." Robb was now pacing back and forth. He acted more and more agitated as he got in Donna's face. "You will be mine."

"What don't you get, I like girls." Donna spat some blood out of her mouth. It landed on his cheek, and she saw a fire ignite in him. "You can't get pussy or something? Gotta stalk a lesbian? You're trash." The words were harsh,

"We can talk about pussy." Robb's eyes showed amusement, and he picked up his knife once more. "Watch this."

Donna watched as Robb took the knife and walked over to Amanda. He knelt in front of her, blocking Donna's view of whatever events were going to happen. His arm moved between the dead woman's legs, and Donna heard a squishing sound. His arm moved in a meticulous fashion, as if he had done this before.

"Almost done, dear…" he said as he glanced back at Donna. "Just a little more." His arm stayed steady as he gave Donna a smile that showed her his excitement.

Donna looked on, watching his body move, wondering what he was doing. Afraid of actually knowing. Her mind raced, trying to figure out how to get loose, trying to not think about what he was going to do to her. She wanted to cry, wanted to mourn the death of her wife, but she had to figure out how to get away before she could really take in anything else.

"Hey look at this!" Robb jumped up and turned around. "Wanna kiss me now?" He laughed. Donna couldn't believe what she was seeing. Robb had cut the skin from Amanda's vagina and had it stuck to his face as he danced around the kitchen. His tongue slid in and out of the hole, making a wet, slurping sound.

Horrified, Donna couldn't control herself. Vomit spewed from her mouth, and she closed her eyes. Her stomach clenched. A moment later, she felt a hand crash into her face as Robb yelled, "Look at me when I'm performing for you, bitch!"

Donna opened her eyes, and he was right in her face. His tongue wiggled at her from behind the skin.

"She was a salty bitch, wasn't she?" He asked Donna. "Give it a lick." He removed the skin from his face and stuck the lips up to Donna's mouth. Donna pulled her head back, tears streaming down her face, and Robb slammed a fist into her stomach. The impact jolted her forward. Her face rubbed against the bloody vagina skin mask, and she gagged.

"We can still have it all you know. The good life. You and me."

He pulled out a pan and turned the stove on. "Are you hungry? I'm starving. Let me cook for you. I am an amazing chef. Let's see, some spices would be good."

He put a little avocado oil in the pan and let it heat up. "Now, this is a new recipe. Hopefully, it's good." He placed the fresh-cut skin in the pan, and it began to sizzle. "Some rosemary, garlic... Do you have a preference for seasonings, dear?" He waited a moment for a response, but Donna gave him none.

"What shall we call this? A clam bake?" He giggled to himself. "Smells amazing, even if I do say so myself." He flipped the meat in the pan. "I take it you like it a little pink inside?"

Donna felt dizzy. Her head was swimming with a million thoughts. She twisted her hands, trying to free her wrists from the rope that held her in place. Her eyes stayed locked on Robb as he shuffled through the cabinets, pulling out plates and utensils.

Robb pulled the meat out of the pan and slapped it on a plate. He took a steak knife and fork and cut off a few pieces. Small, perfect squares that were just the right size.

Grabbing a small piece of skin, he popped it in his mouth, closed his eyes, and smiled. "It's been way too long since I've tasted flesh, and your girl is so good. This just melts in the mouth," Robb smacked a little with his statement as he chewed on the piece of meat. "You have to taste this, Donna. She's so moist." He picked up a piece of meat and walked over to her. "Open up, give this a try."

Donna tried to turn her head away, but he forced the meat into her mouth. She bit down quickly, getting his finger with her teeth. He yanked his hand back, and the skin tore away. Robb pulled his hand back and took a huge swing. All Donna had time to see was his first hurling at her face before her world turned dark.

CHAPTER 15

"Now look at what you've done," Robb said to an unconscious Donna. He lifted her head and stared at her face. Blood oozed from her bottom lip. He took a single finger and wipes away what he could and placed a kiss on her. "I don't think I can forgive you for this, but we'll see if you can make it up to me."

He untied Donna from the chair and retied her hands together behind her back. When he was sure the rope was tight enough, he lifted her and slung her over his shoulder. He hadn't thought this all the way through, but he was sure he could figure out what to do next. He lugged her body out of the house, trying to prepare himself for the long hike back to his truck.

"I don't know if I'm built for this kind of physical activity, Donna."

He shook his head when there was no response. The women in this town had turned out to be a big disappointment. That was the story of his life though, one disappoint after another. Not just with women, with everything from work and money to simple happiness. Something always seemed to get screwed somewhere, and everything fell apart.

Halfway down the path Robb tripped over something and began to tumble. Donna dropped from his grasp and hit the ground with a thud, and he landed right beside her. His breaths were ragged, and he had a hard time breathing. Taking several deep breaths in, he released the air slowly from his burning lungs.

"Why couldn't you love me?" He questioned the woman next to him. "I could have given you everything. Why didn't you want that for yourself?"

There were so many questions in his head that he wanted to ask her, but time was slowly running out. He struggled to his feet and grabbed Donna by the legs. Perhaps dragging her the rest of the way would be easier than carrying her. She didn't deserve an easy trip anyways.

"Onward we go," Robb said as he began to yank Donna the rest of the way. Here and there he could hear the thumping as her head hit the ground. He was sure that by the time they reached the truck the back of her skull would be ripped apart. The thought made him smile.

CHAPTER 16:

BACK TO THE BEGINNING

The blade of the shovel clunked when the metal hit the truck bed. Robb sat on the tailgate, lighting a cigarette. He wiped the sweat away from his face and leaned his head back, eyes staring up at the cloudy night sky. He felt a small drop of water hit his face, and a moment later a downpour began. The filth from his body gathered in large puddles around him, and he stretched his arms out, enjoying the cool. His heart was heavy, but this was a sign of good things to come. He was sure of it.

After several minutes, he stood up and pushed up the tailgate of his truck. There was nothing he could do now except go back to his room at the motel and crash for the night. In the morning, he'd gather his things and head out, to a new town maybe. Somewhere he'd never been, perhaps. Something better than this town, for sure. Some place with people who would appreciate him. It was hard finding good people nowadays. He thought he had found something special with Donna, but he was wrong. Once again.

A cool breeze brushed his skin, and he shivered. "Time to head out, girl. Don't worry though. I'll come visit you from time to time," he said while looking back at the freshly dug grave. He walked to the truck cab and got in. Turning on the radio, he bobbed his head to the rhythm as he pulled away. Next stop, to clean up and get some sleep.

Robb made the trip home quickly, knowing he had work to do before he could leave in the morning, but he needed to make a fairly quick exit. "Maybe I'll just grab stuff and leave tonight," he said to himself. He pulled up in front of the hotel and sat for a moment, trying to decide what he should do.

"Leave now it is." He tapped his fingers on the steering wheel to the beat of the song and waited for it to finish. He slid out of the truck when he was sure no one was around and headed to his room.

Robb fumbled with his keys for a moment, hands still a little shaky from the events of the night. He finally got the door open and walked in, flipping on the light as he closed the door behind him.

Robb jumped when he realized he wasn't alone.

Mary stood in front of him.

"Didn't think you'd see me again, did you?" Mary asked him before something smashed into the back of his head, and everything went black.

CHAPTER 17

Robb blinked a few times and tried to look around. His vision blurred, and he closed his eyes again. His head was killing him. He tried to think back, trying to figure out what happened. Everything seemed fuzzy. He had parted ways with Donna and headed back to the hotel. He was going to leave and then…Mary! How could that be? He had taken care of her. How could she have come back? There's no way she survived.

"Hi there, Robb. Good to see you again." Mary ran her finger down Robb's face to his chest and then stopped. He squirms, trying to get away, but was unable to move. "Don't worry, we made sure you won't be able to get away."

"Fucking bitch." The words spewed from Robb's mouth. "Who's we?"

"Now, now. Don't be angry. You're the one who wanted to play." Mary giggled. "I'm still a little off from our last visit so I asked for some help. Brad was more than happy to…" Robb could see she was trying to choose her next words carefully. "He didn't mind lending an extra hand, since you took mine. Actually, a few of the girls decided to join us."

Robb looked around, trying to figure out where he was. Cement walls and a few metal poles… must be a basement, but where? In the middle of the room, a table was set up with various tools for pleasure and pain.

He tried to wiggle free again, but the rope tying him to one of those poles was tight and rubbed against his naked flesh. He looked around again and saw several familiar faces from the bar.

"Creepy fuck. What did you do to Donna? Where's she at?" Brad asked him.

"Donna was a bad girl. I fixed that." Robb laughed. "Don't worry, those girls have eternity together now."

Brad slammed his fist into the side of Robb's face, and the crunch echoed through the room. He repeated the process several times, and with each hit Robb let out a laugh.

"This stupid son of a bitch is nuts." Brad spat at him. "Where's Donna?"

Robb stopped laughing and became serious. "I can show you, but you'll have to let me go. I'll take you there. She's close to home." He winked at Brad.

"Did you see all the blood at her house? There's no way she's still alive, Brad." Mary responded. "And poor Amanda…"

"She was tasty," Robb interrupted. A grin spread across his face. "Just a few spices and she was a wonderful treat. Juicy and tender…"

"Stop!" Mary screamed. She used her remaining hand and picked up a knife next to her, handing it to one of the girls.

"Cut his tongue out. I don't want to hear from him anymore."

The girl didn't question Mary. She took the knife and walked toward Robb. He opened his mouth and stuck out his tongue. "If you cook it just right, sauté it in some red wine, it's a wonderful delicacy." He said, then stuck it out again.

She turned back to Mary. "I don't know if I can do this. I have a thing with blood."

Brad grabbed hold of Robb's tongue with some pliers and Robb felt him yank hard. He felt the muscle tearing away from the hyoid bone. Tears welled up in Robb's eyes, and Brad grabbed the knife from the girl's hand. In one quick motion, the knife slashed through the meat held in place by the pliers. Part of the tongue dropped to the floor.

Blood flowed from Robbs mouth, and tears ran from his eyes. He still managed a laugh. He refused to let them know his suffering. The loss of his love was torture enough; nothing after that could really hurt him. Right?

Mary picked up the limp piece of meat from the floor. She smiled at Robb, her lips dotted with little red holes from where he had sewn it shut. "With all of the shit that's come out of your mouth, I know where this belongs."

She placed the tongue against his anal opening and slowly pushed up. She plunged her fingers as far as they would go, and he tightened around her. His eyes widened, and his penis jumped a little, then stood at attention.

"This fucker is enjoying it," one of the girls whispered. "Let's see if he enjoys this." She picked up a glove from the table and put it on. He watched as she ran a finger across the palm of the glove to test the roughness of the sandpaper attached to it.

He squirmed more, and she grabbed hold of his erection and rubbed on him a moment. "You'll really like this." A burning sensation hit him as she grabbed him tighter with her gloved hand. He could feel the skin being shredded as she continued to stroke him. His leg began to shake, and he grit his teeth. Blood ran down her hand, and Robb lets out a little grunt. White fluid dripped from the tip of his penis, mixing with the drops of blood beneath him on the floor.

He growled through the pleasure and pain and winced when he looked down at the grated piece of meat hanging limp between his legs.

C H A P T E R   1 8

"I want his arm, Brad. He took mine and now I want his," Mary exclaimed.

"Mary, listen…" Brad began. "He deserves everything he gets, but let's just end this. I want him gone so he can't hurt anyone else. We are all tired and you need to go to the doctor. Let's just end him now."

"He will be gone after I get his arm. And maybe a nipple." Mary's voice was low and ruthless. Brad saw a look in her eyes that he'd never seen before. A brutal hatred for this man. He understood where she was coming from. He was angry as well with what this man had done to her, and he couldn't even imagine what he had done with their friends. For her he would do anything.

Seeing the sorrow and hurt on Mary's face brought forth a burning rage. He never wanted to see this woman in pain. He never wanted to see her sad. She would have whatever she wanted from this man, and he would make sure of that.

Brad picked up a hand saw from the table and handed it to her. "I got you," he said, pumping himself up for the task at hand. "Let's do this." Brad untied the rope just enough to release one of Robb's arms then ties him back, drawing the ropes tighter than before. When he hears Robb curse him he figures the rope is tight enough.

Robb swung his arm, but Brad moved quicker and had control of the situation before anything occurred in Robb's favor. He took the man's wrist and pulled his arm out straight, extending it and giving Mary the best possible angle. With her one arm shaking, she placed the blade of the saw just below Robb's shoulder and took a deep breath.

"This will be a lot slower than when you took my arm. I'm working with a disability now," Mary informed him.

The room grew silent, everyone's eyes watching. The blade of the saw as it ran over Robb's arm, and they could all hear the flesh tear as she slowly added pressure. She worked the tool back and forth until she hit bone. The whole time Robb tried to scream out. It sounded more like a rabid animal with his tongue missing.

"I may need help," Mary said, looking at Brad. "I don't think I have the strength to get through his bone."

"I've got you," Brad replied.

"Take your time. I want to enjoy this," Mary said.

Brad winked at her and took the saw, setting it on the table. He grabbed Robb's arm with both of his hands and ripped down, dislocating the shoulder bone. He dug his fingers into the flesh and began ripping the rest of his arm away from the man's body. A howl erupted from Robbs throat. His body jerked and then went limp.

"Is he dead?" one of the girls asked.

"Not yet," Brad replied. "He's taking a nap."

"We can always bury him alive. Or, like back in the day, put his head on a stake and leave it in the middle of nowhere." Brad turned his head a little sideways, his fingers twisting a section of his beard.

"You might be onto something here. Impale him." He began to untie the man and slung him over his shoulder. They began to climb the stairs and were greeted with the bloody mess Robb had left in Donna's kitchen, with Amanda still attached to the chair. Everyone watched as Mary walked over and whispered to her, taking her hand, and closing her eyes. She then followed the group outside to the shed.

Brad opened the door of the building and entered, leaving everyone else standing at the door. He began rummaging through things. He was searching for something. He knew in his mind what he needed and his eyes scanned every little inch of the shed until he finally spotted it.

He came out with something that looked like a thick wooden skewer and a sledgehammer.

"You girls ready? We can take turns with this," Brad said while giving the girls a sideways glance. He handed the sledgehammer to one of them and placed the sharp end of the post in Robb's mouth. He adjusted the head to create a straighter path.

"All set. Give it a good whack." Within a moment there was a clunk, and the wooden post inched its way down Robb's throat. Brad held the post steady as the girls took turns working the post through the man's body until it finally found its exit point.

"These girls have the best fire pit. It's huge. Can do a lot of stuff with it. And they always had it ready for a good fire." No one was really listening as Brad talked to himself while putting the freshly made Robb-skewer across the fire pit. He checked the wood and doused it with a bottle of lighter fluid that he happened to find sitting next to the large concrete fire slab.

Mary broke out in laughter as he lit it up. Tears welled up in her eyes. "They would appreciate a good BBQ out here. Especially on a night like this."

ABOUT THE AUTHOR

Angelique Jordonna is an author of darkly intense horror, thrillers, and paranormal romance. Her books take you into the depths of depravity while still having elements of the strong love bonds between characters. The rich descriptions pull you right into the story, whether she's detailing a gruesome murder or dropping subtle hints at a burgeoning romance.

Angelique has a love for all things creative, and she devours books and music like they were the finest cuisine, sustaining her better than the finest wines, better than a five-star meal, better than ... sex? Well, maybe not *that* good.

You can find the author on all platforms and check out her website

Angeliquejordonnaauthor.com

ABOUT THE PUBLISHER / EDITOR

Dawn Shea is an author and half of the publishing team over at D&T Publishing. She lives with her family in Mississippi. Always an avid horror lover, she has moved forward with her dreams of writing and publishing those things she loves so much.

Follow her author page on Amazon for all publications she is featured in.

Follow D&T Publishing at their website, **www.dt-publishing.com**, or search for their Facebook Group

Or email here: dandtpublishing20@gmail.com

The Night She Came Back by Angelique Jordonna

Cover by Ruth Anna Evans

Edited by Tasha Schiedel

Formatting by Ash Ericmore